# Big, Terrible Trouble?

By Craig McCracken
Illustrated by Craig McCracken and Lou Romano

Craig McCracken is the creator of the Emmy-nominated animated series,
*The Powerpuff Girls*. He wrote and illustrated this
special collector's edition exclusively for Golden Books.

## A GOLDEN BOOK • NEW YORK
Golden Books Publishing Company, Inc., New York, New York 10106

POWERPUFF GIRLS and all related characters and elements are trademarks of Cartoon Network © 1999.
CARTOON NETWORK and logo are trademarks of Cartoon Network © 1999. All rights reserved. Printed in
China. No part of this book may be reproduced or copied in any form without written permission from
the publisher. GOLDEN BOOKS ®, A GOLDEN BOOK®, A LITTLE GOLDEN BOOK®, G DESIGN®, and the
distinctive gold spine are trademarks of Golden Books Publishing Company, Inc. Library of Congress
Catalog Card Number: 99-067261      ISBN: 0-307-99500-3      A MCMXCIX      First Edition 1999

We'd be happy to answer your questions and hear your comments. Please call us
toll free at 1-888-READ-2-ME (1-888-732-3263). Hours: 8 AM–8 PM EST, weekdays. US and Canada only.

**T**he City of Townsville!
   A safe city protected by the best superheroes ever,
the Powerpuff Girls!

**I**t was a calm and peaceful day as the students of Pokey
Oaks Kindergarten quietly worked on their projects.

Suddenly, the Powerpuff Hotline began to buzz!
"Townsville's in trouble! Let's roll!" commanded
Blossom.
The Powerpuff Girls took to the sky to save the city.

BOOM! CRASH! The Girls burst into the Mayor's office.
"What's the problem, Mayor?" asked Blossom.
"Oh, Girls," cried the Mayor. "It's big, terrible trouble!"
"What? What is it?" demanded Buttercup.
"It's the worst," replied the Mayor.
"Please tell us!" Bubbles pleaded.

Just then the Girls' ultrasonic hearing picked up a faint scream across town. RRRRRRRRRING! The bank alarm!

"Don't worry, Mayor, we know what the problem is," declared Blossom.

And with that, the Girls were on their way.

At the bank, the evil Mojo Jojo was making off with a big bag of loot. But before he could get away . . . BAM! BIFF! POW! The Powerpuff Girls showed him what for!

Back at the Mayor's office, the Girls explained that they took care of that nasty Mojo Jojo and everything was now okay.

"But that wasn't it! Something even more terrible has happened!" exclaimed the Mayor.

"What could be more terrible than Mojo?" the Girls wondered.

Suddenly Bubbles's hypersensitive mood detector
kicked in and she began to feel very sad.
 "I have a feeling there are some helpless creatures
who are very scared right now," she said.
 The Girls took off following Bubbles's lead.

The Girls arrived at the Townsville Mountains to find mean ol' Fuzzy Lumkins going wild.

"Git offa my propity!" hollered Fuzzy as he fired his boomstick at all the helpless critters.

"Your property? The forest is the property of all
who live here," scolded Bubbles as she melted
Fuzzy's boomstick with her heat vision.

"My propity," Fuzzy muttered sadly as he held his
destroyed weapon in his hand.

The Girls returned to the Mayor's office. They all agreed that Fuzzy was worse than Mojo Jojo, but he was all taken care of now.

"Oh, Girls! That wasn't it either! This is something even bigger!" cried the Mayor.

"Bigger? What could be bigger?" questioned Buttercup.

Suddenly . . . BOOM! BOOM! BOOM! The whole building began to rumble!

The Girls looked out the window to see a giant monster destroying Townsville.

"That's bigger all right! C'mon!" called Buttercup as the trio went into action.

It was a tough fight, but the Girls were able to stop the beast from destroying the town they love. Whew! What a tough day of crime fighting for the little superheroes. Even though they were all tuckered out, they returned to the Mayor's office once again to let him know that all was safe.

"So much for the monster!" bragged Buttercup.

"See ya, Mayor," the Girls called as they were about to leave.

"Wait!" called the Mayor. "What about the big, terrible trouble?"

"What about it? We stopped the monster, Fuzzy Lumkins, and Mojo Jojo. What other trouble is there?" they asked.

The Mayor pulled out a big jar and exclaimed . . .
"I can't get my pickle jar open!!"
PLOP! The dumbfounded Girls fell to the floor.

And so once again the day was saved, whether the Mayor thinks so or not! Thanks to the Powerpuff Girls!